THERE'S A BIG, BEAUTIFUL WORLD OUT THERE!

NANCY CARLSON

PUFFIN BOOKS

PUFFIN BOOKS
Published by Penguin Group
Penguin Young Readers Group,
345 Hudson Street, New York, New York 10014, U.S.A.
Penguin Books Ltd, 80 Strand, London WC2R ORL, England
Penguin Books Australia Ltd, 250 Camberwell Road, Camberwell, Victoria 3124, Australia
Penguin Books Canada Ltd, 10 Alcorn Avenue, Toronto, Ontario, Canada M4V 3B2
Penguin Books (N.Z.) Ltd, 182-190 Wairau Road, Auckland 10, New Zealand

First published in the United States of America by Viking, a division of Penguin Putnam Books for Young Readers, 2002
Published by Puffin Books, a division of Penguin Young Readers Group, 2004

1 3 5 7 9 10 8 6 4 2

THE LIBRARY OF CONGRESS HAS CATALOGED THE VIKING EDITION AS FOLLOWS:
Carlson, Nancy.
There's a big, beautiful world out there! / by Nancy Carlson.
p. cm.
Summary: A young girl realizes that, although there are many things to be afraid of in the world, such as a thunderstorm, there is even more to look forward to, such as the rainbow that will follow the storm.
ISBN: 0-670-03580-7 (Hardcover)
[1. Fear–Fiction.] I. Title. PZ7.C21665 Ip 2002 [E]–dc21 2002000637

Puffin Books ISBN 0-14-240184-6

Printed in the United States of America
Set in Life, Claredon
Book designed by Teresa Kietlinski

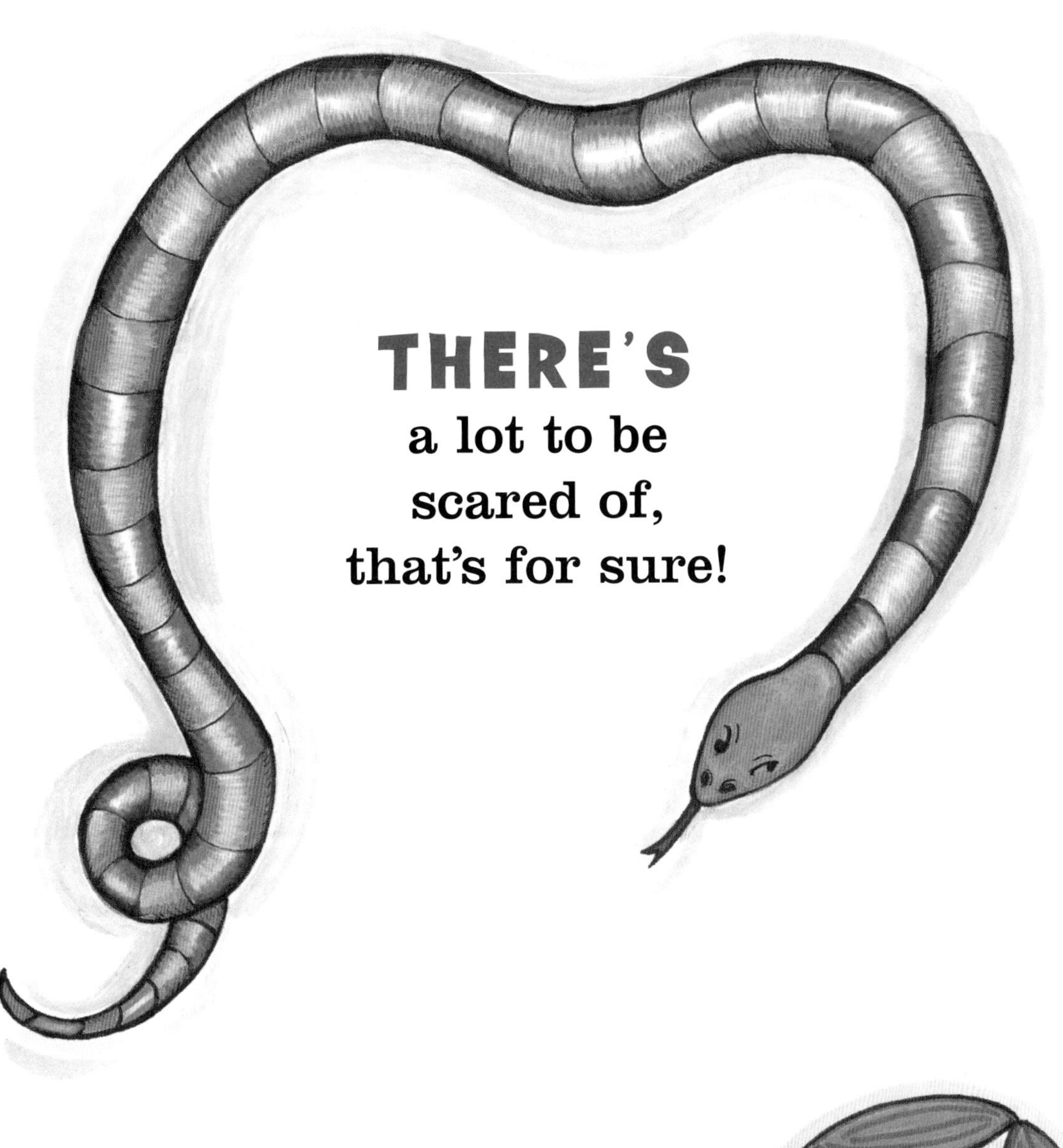

THERE'S
a lot to be
scared of,
that's for sure!

There's that mean-looking dog,

and booming thunderstorms.

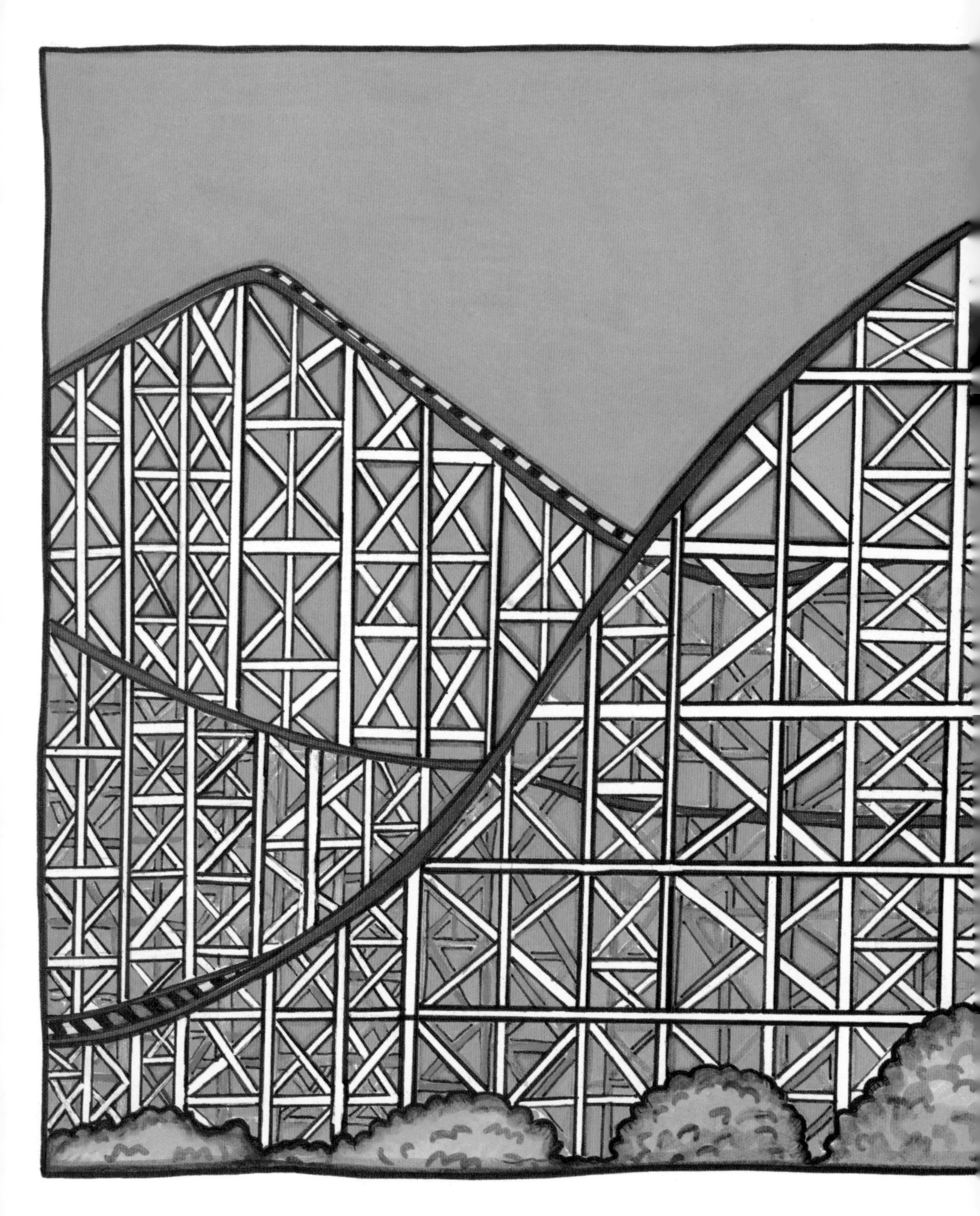

There are roller coasters,

and scary stories in the news.

There's a lot to be scared of, like getting
up in front of a whole bunch of people,

and spiders

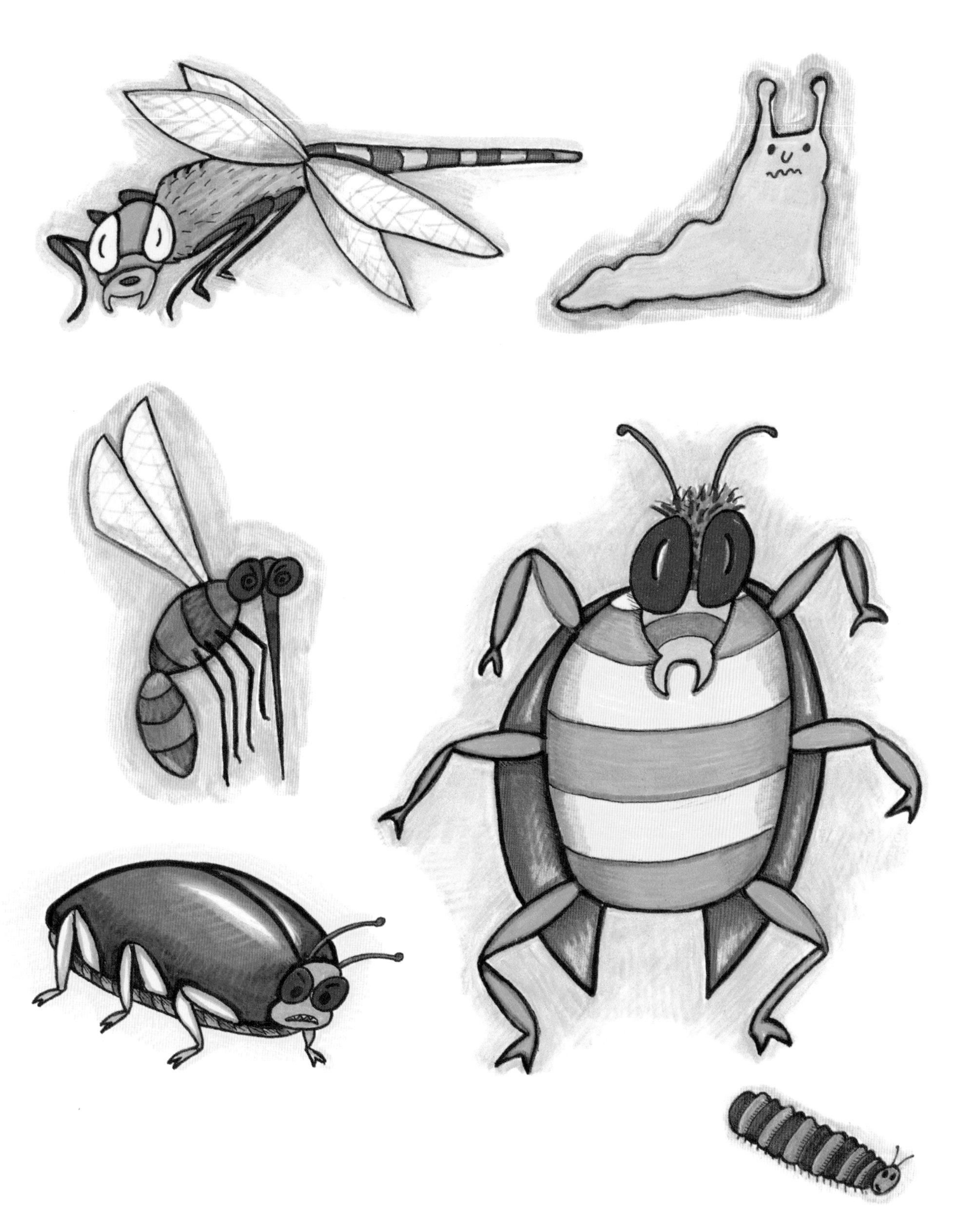

and other creepy crawly things.

There are clowns,

and spooky shadows in your room,

and people who look different from you.

All this scary stuff can make you want to hide under your covers and never come out.

But after a while, hiding under your
covers can get pretty boring.

Maybe that scary dog only looks mean.

If you hide under your covers, you
won't see the rainbow after the storm,

and you might never enjoy
the thrill of the ride!

If you hide under your covers, you'll miss your mother saying everything is going to be all right,

and you might never know how great
you sound singing a solo.

If you hide under your covers, you might not see

all the interesting things in your own backyard.

You'll miss laughing out loud,

and you won't see the stars come out.

And just think of all the new friends

you'll never meet!

There's a lot to be scared of, but there's
even more to look forward to. . . .

So throw off those covers!

There's a big, beautiful world out there

just waiting for you!

This book was written
on September 12, 2001.

IRONDALE PUBLIC LIBRARY
205-951-1415